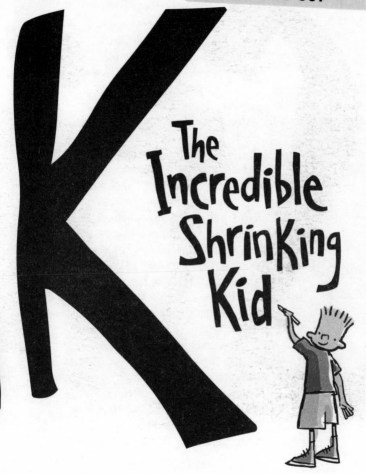

The Incredible Shrinking Kid

Peter H. Reynolds

WALKER BOOKS

Books by Megan McDonald
and Peter H. Reynolds

Judy Moody
Judy Moody Gets Famous!
Judy Moody Saves the World!
Judy Moody Predicts the Future
Judy Moody: The Doctor Is In!
Judy Moody Declares Independence!
Judy Moody: Around the World in 8½ Days
Judy Moody Goes to College
Judy Moody, Girl Detective
Judy Moody and the NOT Bummer Summer
Judy Moody and the Bad Luck Charm
Judy Moody, Mood Martian
Stink: The Incredible Shrinking Kid
Stink and the Incredible Super-Galactic Jawbreaker
Stink and the World's Worst Super-Stinky Sneakers
Stink and the Great Guinea Pig Express
Stink: Solar System Superhero
Stink and the Ultimate Thumb-Wrestling Smackdown
Stink and the Midnight Zombie Walk
Stink and the Freaky Frog Freakout
Stink and the Shark Sleepover
Stink-O-Pedia: Super Stink-y Stuff From A to Zzzzz
Stink-O-Pedia 2: More Stink-y Stuff From A to Z
Judy Moody & Stink: The Holly Joliday
Judy Moody & Stink: The Mad, Mad, Mad,
Mad Treasure Hunt
Judy Moody & Stink: The Big Bad Blackout

Books by Megan McDonald

The Sisters Club • *The Sisters Club: Rule of Three*
The Sisters Club: Cloudy with a Chance of Boys

Books by Peter H. Reynolds

The Dot • *Ish* • *Sky Colour* • *The Smallest Gift of Christmas*

Megan McDonald is the author of the
popular series starring Stink's sister, Judy Moody.
She says, "Once, while I was visiting a class, the kids
chanted, 'Stink! Stink! Stink!' as I entered the room.
In that moment, I knew that Stink had to have a
book of his own." Stink now has his very own series.
Megan McDonald lives in California.

You can find out more about Megan McDonald
and her books at **www.meganmcdonald.net**

Peter H. Reynolds is the illustrator of all
the Judy Moody and Stink books. He says, "Stink
reminds me of myself growing up: dealing with a
sister prone to teasing and bossing around – and
having to get creative in order to stand tall beside
her." Peter H. Reynolds lives in Massachusetts.

You can find out more about Peter H. Reynolds
and his art at **www.fablevision.com**

Stir

Megan McDonald   illustrated by

for all the readers who asked for Stink.

M. M.

To the Gary Stager, members of the
Multimedia House of Pancakes, and
every Hotdog-on-a-Stick employee
past, present and future.

P. H. R.

First published 2006 by Walker Books Ltd
87 Vauxhall Walk, London SE11 5HJ

This edition published 2013

4 5 6 7 8 9 10

Text © 2005 Megan McDonald
Illustrations © 2005 Peter H. Reynolds

Stink ™. Stink is a registered trademark of
Candlewick Press, Inc, Somerville MA

The right of Megan McDonald and Peter H. Reynolds to be identified
as author and illustrator respectively of this work has been asserted by them
in accordance with the Copyright, Designs and Patents Act 1988

This book has been typeset in Stone Informal

Printed and bound in Great Britain by Clays Ltd, St Ives plc

British Library Cataloguing in Publication Data:
a catalogue record for this book is available from the British Library

ISBN 978-1-4063-4669-5

www.stinkmoody.com
www.walker.co.uk

CONTENTS

SHORT, SHORTER, SHORTEST

Shrimp-o!

Runtsville!

Shorty Pants!

Stink was short. Short, shorter, shortest. Short as an inchworm. Short as a ... stinkbug!

Stink was the shortest one in the Moody family (except for Mouse, the cat). The shortest second grader in Class 2D. Probably the shortest human being in the whole world, *including Alaska and Hawaii*. Stink was one whole head shorter than his sister, Judy Moody. Every morning he made Judy measure him. And every morning it was the same.

One metre, twelve centimetres tall.

Shrimpsville.

He had not grown one inch. Not one centimetre. Not one hair.

He was always one head shorter than Judy. "I need another head," he told his mum and dad.

"What for?" asked Dad.

"I like your head just the way it is," said Mum.

"You need a new *brain*," said Judy.

"I have to get taller," said Stink. "How can I get taller?"

"Eat your peas," said Dad.

"Drink your milk," said Mum.

"Eat more seafood!" said Judy.

"Seafood?"

"Yes – *shrimp*!" Judy said.

"Hardee-har-har," said Stink. His sister thought she was so funny.

"What's so bad about being short?" asked Dad.

"I have to drink at the baby fountain," said Stink. "And stand in the front row for class pictures. And I always have to be a mouse in school plays. Just once, I'd like a speaking part, not a *squeaking* part."

"Being short isn't all bad," said Dad. "You still get those free colouring books you like at the doctor's."

"And the Spider-Man pyjamas you love still fit you," said Mum.

"And you still get to use your baby step stool just to brush your teeth," said Judy. Stink rolled his eyes.

"You'll grow," said Dad.

"Growing takes time," said Mum.

"Lie down on the floor," Judy told him.

"What for?"

"If I pull your arms, and Mum and Dad each take a leg, we could stretch you out like a rubber band. Then you'd be taller."

Stink did not want to be a rubber band. So he ate all his peas at dinner. He did not hide even one in his napkin. He drank all his milk, and did not pour even one drop into Judy's glass when she wasn't looking.

✳ ✳ ✳

"Measure me again," Stink said to Judy. "One more time. Before bed."

"Stink, I just measured you this morning."

"That was before I ate all those peas and drank all that milk," said Stink.

Stink put on his shoes. He stood next to the Shrimp-O-Meter. He stood up straight. He stood up tall.

Judy got out her Elizabeth Blackwell Women of Science ruler. "Hey, no shoes!" she said. Stink took off his shoes. He stood on tiptoe.

"No tippy-toes either."

Judy measured Stink top to bottom. She measured him foot to head. She measured him head to foot. Something was not right.

"Well?" asked Stink.

"Bad news," said Judy.

"What?" asked Stink.

"You're shorter than you were this morning. Half a centimetre shorter!"

Stink made a face. "Not possible."

"Stink. The Women of Science ruler does not lie."

"Shorter? How can I be shorter?"

"Simple," said Judy. "You shrank!"

"You'll grow," said Dad.

"You'll grow," said Mum.

"But you'll never, ever, *ever* catch up with me!" said Judy.

The Adventures of Stink
in Shrink Monster

BY STINK MOODY

The horrible Shrink Monster attacks the City of Moodyville!

ZAP!
EEEEK!

BEFORE
ZAP!

AFTER

Stink, the bravest (and shortest) kid in Moodyville, confronts the Shrink Monster!

GRRRRRR!
STOP!

ZAP
Huh?

Stink shrunk!

Max, fetch the Stink-Mobile.

Good boy, Max.

Will Stink have enough time to invent an un-shrinker? Or will Stink be attending Molecule Elementary School?

Stink-Mobile

SHRINK, SHRANK, SHRUNK

When Stink woke up the next morning, his bed felt as big as a country. The ceiling was up there with the sky. And it was a long way down to the floor.

When he went to brush his teeth, even the sink seemed too tall.

"Yikes! I really am shrinking," said Stink, checking himself out in the mirror. Were his arms a little shorter? Was his head a little smaller?

Stink got dressed. He put on up-and-down-striped trousers and an up-and-down-striped shirt.

"What's with the stripes?" asked Judy.

"Makes me look taller," said Stink.

"If you say so," said Judy.

"What?"

"If you really want to look taller, here's what you do." Judy handed him a fancy shampoo-type bottle. "Put this hair gel on your hair and leave it in for ten minutes. Then you'll be able to comb your hair so it sticks straight up. Sticking-up hair will make you look taller."

Stink put the gooey gloop in his hair. He left it in his hair while he made his bed. He left it in his hair while he packed up his backpack. He left it in his hair all through breakfast.

"We could play baseball, and you could be *short*stop," Judy told him.

"So funny I forgot to laugh," said Stink.

Judy pointed to Stink's hair. "Hey, I think it's working!" she said.

"Really? Do you think people will notice?"

"They'll notice," said Judy.

Stink ran upstairs to look in the mirror. "HEY! My HAIR! It's ORANGE!"

"Don't worry," said Judy. "It'll wash out … in about a week."

"I look like a carrot!" said Stink.

"Carrots are tall," said Judy, and she laughed all the way to the bus stop.

∗ ∗ ∗

Stink's friend Elizabeth sat next to him in class. They were the shortest kids in Class 2D, so they sat at the front. "Hi, Elizabeth," said Stink.

"I'm not Elizabeth any more," she told Stink. "From now on, call me Sophie of the Elves."

"OK. I have a new name, too. The Incredible Shrinking Stink."

"But, Stink, you look taller today," said Elizabeth.

"It's just the hair," said Stink. "I'm still short."

"Not to an elf. To an elf, you'd be a giant. To an elf, you would be the Elf King."

"Thanks, Sophie of the Elves," said Stink.

The bell rang, and Mrs Dempster passed out spelling words. Three of the new words were *shrink*, *shrank*, *shrunk*. At lunch, the dessert was strawberry *short*cake. And in Reading, Mrs Dempster read everybody a book called *The Shrinking of Treehorn*.

The book was all about a boy who plays games and reads cereal boxes and gets shorter and shorter. He keeps shrinking and shrinking. Then, just when he becomes a normal size again, he turns green!

"Any comments?" Mrs Dempster asked when the story was over.

Stink raised his hand. "Is that a true story?"

Mrs D. laughed. "I'm afraid not," she said. "It's fantasy."

"Fantasy's my favourite!" said Sophie of the Elves. "Especially hobbits and elves."

"Are you sure it's fantasy?" asked Stink. "Because that kid is a lot like me. Because I'm ... I'm..." Stink could not make himself say *shrinking*.

"Because you both turned another colour?" asked Webster.

"Um, because I like to read everything on the cereal box, too," said Stink.

"OK," said Mrs Dempster. "Let's see. Who's going to carry the milk from the canteen today?" Stink was barely paying attention. He never got asked to carry the milk.

"How about Mr James Moody?" asked Mrs Dempster.

"Me?" asked Stink. He sat up taller. "I get to carry the milk?"

Stink walked down the second grade corridor. It looked longer than usual. And wider. He took the stairs down to the canteen. Were there always this many stairs? His legs felt shorter. Like they shrink, shrank, shrunk.

Stink got the milk crate. He carried the milk up the stairs, past the office, and past the staff room. Now his arms felt shorter. He needed a rest. He set the milk down outside the nurse's office.

"Hi, Stink!" called Mrs Bell. "I see you have a new hairstyle."

"My sister turned it ORANGE," said Stink.

"So, what brings you here today? Headache? Sore throat? There's a lot going around, you know."

"Is shrinking going around?" asked Stink. "Because I think I'm shrinking.

As in getting shorter."

"You're shrinking? What makes you think so?"

"My sister. I mean, she measures me every morning. And I'm always one metre, twelve centimetres. But last night she measured me before I went to bed, and I'd shrunk! I was only one metre, eleven and a half centimetres. I'm a whole half a centimetre shorter!"

"Don't worry, honey," said Mrs Bell. "Everybody shrinks during the day. We're all a little shorter at night than we are in the morning."

"Seriously?"

"Seriously. From gravity, and all the walking around we do, the pads between our bones shrink during the day. At night they soak up water and expand again."

"We all shrink?" asked Stink.

"That's what I'm saying. Everybody shrinks."

"Scientific!" said Stink.

The Adventures of Stink
in King of the Elves

BY STINK MOODY

Beautiful Sophie of the Elves falls under the dreaded gravity spell.

An evil witch pours hex-mix in Sophie's trainers.

My feet feel sooo HEAVY...

POOF!

TA-DA! Stink, King of the Elves, arrives!

Not a minute to lose!

ANTI-GRAVITY SOAKING CHAMBER 1 MILE→

THERE!

30 SECONDS LATER...

My hero!

A larger-than-life statue to thank you, Stink!

STINK King of the Elves

UP, UP, UP

Stink walked tall down the corridor, around the corner, and back to class 2D.

"Stink! You won!" said Sophie of the Elves.

"While you were gone," said Mrs Dempster, "we drew a name to see who would get to take Newton home this weekend. Your name was chosen."

"For real? Me? I get to take the newt home?"

"You have all the luck," said Webster.

"Things are definitely looking up, up, UP," said Stink, telling himself a joke and cracking himself up, up, up.

* * *

Stink climbed on the bus. He held the Critter Keeper carefully in his lap. "Don't worry, Newton," said Stink. "I'll take really good care of you. The best."

"What's that?" asked Judy when she got on the bus.

"A red-spotted newt. Like a baby salamander. His name's Newton."

"Where'd you get him?"

"He's our class pet. We're studying life-cycles, and Mrs D. went to New Hamster and brought him back for us. I'm taking care of him for the weekend. I get to play with him and watch him and keep a journal of stuff that happens."

Judy snorted. "New *Hampshire*, Stink. Not New Hamster."

"You mean *Newt* Hampshire!" said Judy's friend Rocky.

"It's in *Newt* England," said Judy, cracking up. Stink rolled his eyes.

* * *

When Stink got home, he did not stop to get a snack. Not even Fig *Newtons*. He took Newton up to his room. He got out his notebook and wrote:

friday 3:37 Newton hiding

Stink stared at the newt. Judy came in and peered over his shoulder.

friday 3:40 Newton hiding

friday 3:45 Newton still hiding

"You should write BORING in your journal," said Judy.

"Newts are not boring," said Stink.

"Name one UN-boring thing about a newt," said Judy.

"Newts eat crickets. And worms and slugs," said Stink.

"BOR-ing!" said Judy.

"Red-spotted newts are the state amphibian of New Hampshire."

"BOR-ing," said Judy.

"OK. How about this? Newts start out as eggs. Then they hatch and swim around like tadpoles. Then they turn into red newts and live on land. Then they change colour and go back into the water."

"Now that's a teensy-weensy bit not-boring," said Judy.

"And they shed their skins," Stink said.

"Interesting!" said Judy. "Call me when *that* happens."

* * *

On Saturday, Stink wrote in his journal some more.

10:52	Newton sniffed at worm
10:53	Newton sniffed at fake turtle
11:00	Newton ate cricket — whole!
11:30	Newton climbed up on new rock
11:36	Misted Newton with spray bottle
11:38	Newton stared at magazine picture of pond
11:45	Newton sleeping
12:00	Newton hiding
12:06	Still hiding

"Stink, are you going to stare at that newt all weekend?" asked Judy.

"I'm building him a raft. Out of Lego. Maybe he'll come out and float."

"You know what would be really UN-boring?" asked Judy. "Put the newt in with Toady."

"No way!" said Stink. "Newts are like poison to toads."

"So that means Toady won't eat him. C'mon, Stinker. Toady's all lonely." Before Stink could say Fig Newton, Judy scooped up Newton in her hands.

"You're supposed to wash your hands," said Stink. "Don't drop him."

"I won't drop him." She set him down on some moss in Toady's tank.

Newton sniffed at Toady and curled up his tail. "He's scared!" said Stink.

"Wait," said Judy. Toady licked Newton.

"Take him out!" yelled Stink.

"It was just a friendly lick," said Judy. "A newt lollipop."

"What if Toady gets poisoned? Get him out. Get him out!"

"Don't lay an egg!" Judy picked up Newton in her not-washed hand. "Stink! Something bad is happening to Newton. His head is splitting open."

"Let me see!" Stink peered at the

newt. Sure enough, Newton's skin had split, starting right at his head.

"He's shedding his skin!" said Stink. "Put him back! Put him back!"

They peered at Newton. "Do you think it'll really come off?" asked Stink.

"Sure," said Judy. "It means he's growing. Unlike *some* people."

"Even a newt grows more than me," said Stink.

"BOR-ing. I wish something would happen," said Judy. She leaned over and wrote in Stink's journal:

1:15 Boring!

Stink erased it. "Growing takes time," he told Judy. "That's what everybody always tells me."

"Maybe if we say some magic words," said Judy.

"Eye of newt,
Blah blah blah,
Wool of bat,
Tongue of toad."

"It's happening!" said Stink.

"Rare!" said Judy. She ran to get the video camera. "Lights! Camera! Action!" Stink took out his journal and wrote:

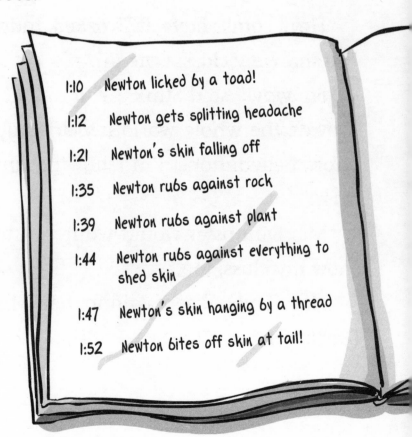

1:10	Newton licked by a toad!
1:12	Newton gets splitting headache
1:21	Newton's skin falling off
1:35	Newton rubs against rock
1:39	Newton rubs against plant
1:44	Newton rubs against everything to shed skin
1:47	Newton's skin hanging by a thread
1:52	Newton bites off skin at tail!

"Gross!" said Judy. She stopped the camera.

"Sweet!" said Stink, staring at the newt skin.

"Hey, can I have it?" asked Judy. "To show my class, I mean?"

"No way!" said Stink. "You already showed the whole world my dried-up baby bellybutton. I'm showing *my* class."

"Mrs Dumpster would want you to show my class, too."

"Not if you keep calling her Mrs Dumpster."

The Adventures of Stink in Newt Boy

by Stink Moody

Stink Moody stumbles upon a supersonic newt skin!

Stinkerbell, Shrinkerbell

P.U.! What's that smell?" Judy held her nose.

"What smell?"

"That dead-skunk smell. That one-hundred-year-old-dirty-sock smell. That three-hundred-year-old-rotten-egg smell." Judy walked around Stink's room, sniffing here, sniffing there. "It gets super-stinky as soon as you get close to Newton."

"Newton!" cried Stink. He sprang up from the floor, where he'd been drawing comics. Newton was in his hidey-hole. "Maybe it's the chopped-up dead worms in there. And dried-up crickets. Why isn't he eating?"

"Grody, grody, gross! There's green-y slime everywhere," Judy said.

"And brown stuff floating in the water."

"Stink, you have to clean it every day. Newts can die if their water gets too dirty."

"Since when are you the newt genius?"

"Since I read it in *Newtsweek*

magazine. You have to dump out the yucky water and wash the rocks and clean off all the slime and stuff."

"That's a lot of homework!" Stink said.

"C'mon, Stinkerbell. I'll help. We'll be the Slime Busters."

"Slime Busters! Double cool!" said Stink. "But you can't call me Stinkerbell."

"If you say so, Stinkerbell. Let's take it down to the big sink." Stink carried the Critter Keeper down to the kitchen, but he couldn't reach the sink.

"Here, let me," said Judy. She took the Critter Keeper from Stink and set it on the counter. Stink stood on a kitchen chair.

"First we have to get Newton out so we can clean his house. Stink, hold this jar. Let's put Newton in there."

"OK," said Stink, holding a tiny net. Judy reached in to scoop out Newton with her hand.

"The net!" cried Stink. "Mrs D. says use the net for scooping him out."

"Hold on. Wait. I almost have him. Ha, ha!" said Judy. "Gotcha, you little newt-brain!"

"He is not a newt-brain," said Stink. "And ... you're scaring him."

"He sure is slippery," said Judy. "You should call him Squirmy."

Just then, Squirmy squirmed right out of Judy's hand, slipped into the sink and went *SLOOP!* right down the drain.

"Newton!" cried Stink. "You LOST him!" he yelled at Judy.

"Don't worry, Stink," said Judy. "He's probably just swimming around down there under the sink." Judy peered down the drain.

"Is he there?" asked Stink. "Do you see him?"

"I can't see," said Judy. "It's dark... I need a flashlight or something. No. Wait. Let me turn the light on."

Judy flicked the switch over the sink. *GRRRRRRR!* A loud, grinding-up sound made them both jump back.

"STOP!" yelled Stink.

Judy turned off the switch. "Oops. Wrong switch."

"You killed Newton!" cried Stink. "The state amphibian of New Hampshire. My class pet. My homework!"

Stink ran to his room. He threw himself face down on the bed.

Newton was gone. Gone, *goner*, gon*est*. All that was left of Stink's class pet was his not-boring newt skin.

Stink gave the newt skin a place of honour on his desk. Right next to his gold Sacagawea dollar, his state quarters, and his French cootie catcher.

The newt skin just sat there. Lonely. Empty. Dead.

Deader than a doorknob.

Stink decided to do his homework. Homework always made him feel better.

Stink drew a still life of the newt skin for art class. He read a poem called "Who Has Seen the Wind?" He wrote one called "Who Has Seen the Newt?" and he used all his homework phrases in sentences.

Taking care of a newt is **easier said than done.**

*I hope Newton does not **get cold feet** out on the river.*

*If your class pet goes down the drain, **go back to the drawing board.***

Judy came up to his room. "I'm sorry, Stink," she said. "I'm super-duper sorry. But I bet Newton slipped right down the pipes and on down to the river before I even flipped the switch."

Stink put down his pencil. "You think?"

"Newton is having the time of his

life. Think of it like *Stuart Little*. He's probably sailing down the river right now on a raft, having a big, fat, newt adventure."

"What am I going to tell Mrs Dempster? And my class?"

"They'll understand. It's all part of the life-cycle, Stink."

"The garbage disposal is NOT part of the life-cycle!" said Stink.

Stink finished his homework. He wrote the last entry in his journal.

Sunday 5:21 NEWTON GOES DOWN THE DRAIN

The Famous Jameses

On Monday morning, when Stink told Mrs D. about the GDI (Garbage Disposal Incident), she said, "Let's just tell the class Newton ran away. It'll be our little secret." She wasn't even angry. She told Stink she was going back to New Hampshire for Presidents' Day weekend, and she could get another newt.

Class 2D wrote stories about the adventures they thought Newton was having in the big, wide world. Webster wrote about Newton joining a baseball team called the Newt York Yankees. Sophie of the Elves wrote about a magic kingdom where Princess Salamandra was under an evil spell and a newt in shining armour came to rescue her. And Stink wrote about Newton sailing down the river on a raft to Legoland and riding the roller coaster.

The stories made everybody feel much better. Especially Stink. Mrs D.

even told Stink he could keep Newton's skin. As in, for real. For good. For *ever*.

✶   ✶   ✶

Mrs Dempster talked about Presidents' Day for the rest of the week. Stink's class made cotton-wool-ball portraits of George Washington. They made milk-carton-and-pretzel-stick log cabins in honour of Abraham Lincoln. Everybody said how tall Abe was. How tall his hat was. Tall, tall, tall. They acted like Abraham Lincoln was a giant.

"What's so great about living in a log cabin?" Stink asked Webster.

"Lincoln carved his maths problems on the walls, right in the logs."

"He should have got in trouble for writing on the walls!" Stink said.

All week, nobody said a word about Stink's favourite president, James Madison. Not one peep. James Madison had a birthday, too. March 16.

Mrs Dempster told the class, "OK, 2D. Homework is on the board."

What does Presidents' Day mean to you?

"I know! I know!" said Calvin.

"Presidents' Day means you see flags."

"It means we don't have school on Monday," said Webster.

"It means you can buy stuff on sale, because presidents are on money," said Heather S.

"Let's not give away all our ideas," said Mrs D. "I want everybody to write one page about what Presidents' Day means to *you*."

"Can we draw something, too?" asked Lucy.

"Can we write a poem?" asked Sophie of the Elves.

"Can we dress up?" asked Stink.

"Yes, yes, and yes," his teacher said. "But I still want my one page."

Stink took out his Big Head book of presidents. He flipped to the best president ever. President number four, James Madison.

Stink and James Madison were very alike. James Madison was from Virginia. Stink was from Virginia. James Madison had the name James. Stink had the name James! James Madison wore trousers. Stink wore trousers! Same-same!

More people should know about James Madison. They should have a statue of James Madison in the park. Or carve his head on the side of Mt Trashmore. They should sing about him in the state song.

That gave Stink an idea. A great big Presidents' Day idea.

✹ ✹ ✹

All the way home from school, Stink made up words for the state song. He sang it to the tune of *Frère Jacques*. He sang it for Mum. He sang it for Dad.

> *"Ja-ames Mad-i-son*
> *Ja-ames Mad-i-son*
> *Num-ber four, num-ber four*
> *Changed his hair to white*
> *Wrote the Bill of Rights*
> *Ding, dang, dong*
> *We love you."*

"That's great!" said Mum. "I don't think we have a Virginia state song."

"There's a state bird. And a state flower," said Dad.

"And a Virginia state quarter," said Judy.

State quarter! Of course! Lincoln was on a penny. Washington was on a dollar. James Madison should be on the Virginia state quarter!

"Can I use your smelly markers?" Stink asked Judy.

"No," said Judy. "You never put the caps back on."

"Newton," said Stink. "N-E-W-T-O-N.

Poor little newt. *GRRRRRRR.*" Stink made a garbage disposal noise.

"Oh, go ahead," said Judy. "But that's IT. I'm not going to let you keep pulling a NEWTON on me!"

Stink sniffed a grape marker. He sniffed a blueberry marker. He sniffed a black liquorice marker. *Yum, yum!*

He drew an outline of James Madison's head. On either side of it, he drew a quill pen and a number 4. Below it he wrote *E Pluribus Constitution*.

Then he wrote a letter to the governor.

James Madison

Dear Mr Governor,

You should make a James Madison Virginia state quarter. James Madison is way better than ships. Please tell me when you make the new quarter.

I am in second grade at Virginia Dare School. I have a bossy big sister and a cat named Mouse and I had a newt that reached the end of his life-cycle.

Signed,

James E. Moody

P.S. Did you know you are governor of a state with no song?

Tumble, Fluff, Shrink!

Mum! Stink's doing homework again!"
Judy said.

"You can't tell on me for doing homework," said Stink.

"Homework, schmome-work. Let's do something good."

"My homework's good."

"What's your homework?" asked Mum.

"Presidents' Day."

"You're not dressing up as a human flag again, are you?" asked Judy.

"No. I have to tell what Presidents' Day means to me."

"Stink, everybody knows what Presidents' Day means. Presidents' Day means your teacher reads you a book about George Washington's teeth and Abraham Lincoln's beard. Presidents' Day means you make stuff out of lollipop sticks, like a log cabin or a flag."

"Nuh-uh," said Stink.

"Presidents' Day means you draw three circles. One for Lincoln, one for Washington, and one in the middle for the stuff that's the same about both."

"It's called a Venn diagram," Mum said.

"My homework is what it means to *me*. Not what it means to Mr Venn."

"Good for you," Mum said. "What *does* Presidents' Day mean to *you*?"

"Two words," said Stink.

"Washington and Lincoln," said Judy.

"James Madison," said Stink.

Stink got out a bag of cotton wool balls. Stink made an old-timey James Madison wig. Judy helped him glue cotton wool balls to her old Brownie cap.

"Pass the glue," said Stink. "Quit hogging."

"Not so much!" said Judy. Stink didn't listen. He just kept gluing more cotton wool balls. "Let's see how it looks," said Stink.

"It has to dry first, or all the cotton wool balls will fall off," Judy told him.

"Let's dry it in the tumble dryer, then," Stink said.

"Genius!" said Judy.

Stink put the wig in the dryer. "Press START," said Stink. "I can't reach."

Judy pressed the fluff-and-tumble button. They waited. *Ga-lump, ga-lump*. They waited some more. The buzzer went off. *"Voilà!"* said Judy, pulling out the wig.

"YIKES!" yelled Stink. "I said press START. Not SHRINK. Now it looks like ... an elf wig. An *ant* wig."

"YOU put it in the dryer," said Judy.

"YOU pressed the button," said Stink.

"Never mind. We can put powder in your hair. Like James Madison."

"You mean *I* can put powder in my

hair," said Stink. "Just to make sure it doesn't turn orange or anything."

"BOR-ing," said Judy.

✳ ✳ ✳

On Friday, Webster read his report aloud first. It was about making red, white and blue potholders at his grandpa's nursing home on Presidents' Day.

"Presidents' Day means to me that we should have a girl president," said Sophie of the Elves. "Since we don't, I wrote a poem about a First Lady. Stink told me about her, and I found out more. Her name is Dolley Madison."

Dolley Madison, first to be called First Lady.

On a fifteen-cent stamp.

Liked to dance and fish and cook and ride horses.

Looked like a queen.

Easter egg hunt, started it.

Yum! Cupcakes are named after her.

Married James Madison.

Always won running races.

Died in 1849.

Ice cream always dessert at the White House.

Saved a painting of George Washington from a fire.

Ostrich feathers in her hats.

Nice lady!

Last of all was Stink. He wore black. He pinned a number 4 to his shirt. He put white powder all over his hair.

WHAT PRESIDENTS' DAY MEANS TO ME

by James Moody

James Madison was the shortest president ever. He was only one metre, sixty-two centimetres tall, but he did great things.

Presidents' Day means we should not forget about the shortest president ever, James Madison. Everybody knows the tallest. But nobody knows the shortest. He was called "little Apple-John". They said he was "no bigger than a half piece of soap". That's a quote.

If you want to be president, it's good if your name is James. There are a lot of famous Jameses.

"Hey! Your real name is James, too," said Webster.

"Exactly." Stink grinned. He finished reading his report.

Six presidents had the name James, so it must be lucky. James Madison had the name James. He was clever. He wrote the Bill of Rights. He was Father of the Constitution.

James Madison had eight brothers and sisters. If you're president, you get to boss even your big sister. He wore black. He put white powder in his hair to look older. He liked ice cream. He had a pet parrot. No lie. He loved science stuff, like the insides of rabbits. If James Madison was alive, he'd be over 250 years old.

My report is short because James Madison was short, too.

James Madison should be a quarter. James Madison should be a day off.

The End

The Adventures of Stink

in The Return of the Shrink Monster by STINK MOODY

The Shrink Monster is back and he's MAD!

GRRRR!!

GULP!

What a headache!

He's about to throw Stink into the supersonic tumble dryer to shrink him to nothing!

But Stink pushes the Monster into the dryer instead!

Stink pushes the button...

ON

He watches the monster SHRINK...

into a ball of lint!

President James Madison presents Stink with a medal and reward money!

$

yay, stink!

Tall, Taller, Tallest

It was Not-James-Madison-Day on Monday. No school. Judy poked her head into Stink's room. "Stink, I'm supposed to be nice to you."

"Did Mum say?"

"Yep."

"Because of the newt?"

"Yep. And I'm supposed to make you feel taller or something. So, Stinkerbell, how about a birthday party?"

"A birthday party? For who?"

"Come downstairs and see."

Stink raced down the steps, two at a time.

Mum brought out twenty cupcakes on a big plate. They each had a letter on them, and all together, they spelled HAPPY JAMES MADISON DAY.

Dad lit the candles.

Everybody sang the James Madison State Song. Stink blew out all twenty candles. He ate an *M*, an *A*, and half of a *D*. Two and a half cupcakes!

"Presents!" said Judy.

"Presents? It's not even anybody's real birthday," said Stink.

"It's James Madison's un-birthday," said Judy.

"Dad and I made you a card," said Mum. "A Presidents' Day card."

"It was kind of short notice," said Dad. "So we printed some stuff off the Internet." Stink opened the card. It had pictures of short people.

James Madison
PRESIDENT
1m 62cm

Yuri Gagarin
COSMONAUT
1m 57cm

Queen Victoria
MONARCH
1m 52cm

Short Sleeve
Sampson
WRESTLER
1m 27cm

YOU'RE ONLY AS SHORT AS YOU FEEL! Love M+D

At the bottom of the card, Mum and Dad had printed in big letters:

YOU'RE ONLY AS SHORT AS YOU FEEL!

"I found the famous Wrestler Guy," said Judy.

"Thanks!" said Stink.

"Now mine," Judy said. Stink ripped it open. "It's a fun mirror!" Judy told him. "From Rocky's old magic kit. I made it into a presidents mirror. One side is the James Madison side and the other is the Abraham Lincoln side."

Stink looked at himself in the James Madison side of the mirror. He looked super-shrimpy, and wide as a warthog. Everybody cracked up.

"Try the other side!" said Judy. Now

Stink looked as skinny as a pencil and as tall as Abe Lincoln.

"UN-Presidents' Day is better than Presidents' Day any time," said Stink. "WOW backward!"

"W-O-W backward is *wow*, too," said Judy.

"Exactly," said Stink.

"Thanks, you guys," said Stink. "For the cupcakes and presents and stuff."

"The James Madison party was Judy's idea," said Dad.

"Yeah. Are you feeling any taller yet?" Judy asked.

"Maybe a little. Especially when I look in the Abe Lincoln mirror!"

"You know, you weren't always short," said Dad.

"Really?" asked Stink.

"Really?" asked Judy.

"You weren't short when you were a baby," said Mum. "You were long. Fifty-five centimetres long."

"What about me?" asked Judy.

"You were only about forty-eight centimetres," said Dad.

"HA!" said Stink. "You mean *I* was taller than *Judy* when I was born?"

"I guess you could say that," said Mum.

"HA, HA!" Stink elbowed Judy. "Shorty Pants!"

"ROAR!" said Judy.

"More cupcakes, anyone?" Mum asked. "Oops. Almost forgot. An envelope came for you, Stink. Special delivery. Looks like it's from the governor." Mum handed Stink the envelope.

"Open it! Read it out loud!" said Judy.

Stink read the letter.

Dear Mr James Moody,

Thank you kindly for your thoughts concerning the James Madison state quarter. Unfortunately, Virginia has already completed its state quarter programme. We have no plans to issue another one at present. However, we do appreciate your enthusiasm for our forefather James Madison. Did you know that James Madison has been featured on a US half dollar and also on a five-thousand-dollar bill?

Enclosed please find the James Madison Bronze Peace and Friendship Medal in honour of your interest in our fourth president.

Your Governor,
Jean MacDonald

"A five-thousand-dollar bill!" said Stink. "Double, triple, quadruple cool!"

The medal was a copper-coloured coin in a plastic case. On one side it said *James Madison, President of the United States, 1809*. On the other, it had a picture of two hands shaking in friendship.

Stink passed around his brand-spanking-new James Madison friendship coin for everybody to see. While his family "oohed" and "aahed", Stink picked up the presidents mirror. He turned it to the tall side and looked at his reflection.

Everybody says growing takes time, thought Stink. *It's all part of the life-cycle. One day, it's going to happen to me. Me! Mr James Moody!*

In the mood for Stink's older sister Judy Moody?

Then try these!